MW00935598

Dedication: To my son Conner, "Dad, tell me a story about ghosts…and firemen!"

Firehouse No. 9

written by Colin Barry Osborne
illustrations by Lucy Belle

Chapter 1

Conner Richman lived with his Mom and Grandpa
in a little frame house with green shutters and an old
bird bath in the front yard that his Grandpa always made
sure was full of fresh water. Conner's street ran along a
quiet creek that flowed gently through the middle of the
neighborhood before emptying into a small, community
lake. Like most boys would, Conner saw the creek as an
extension of his own front yard. He spent hours playing
along the creek bed, running up and down the banks,

splashing in the shallow water, and looking for all the kinds of things that drift along creeks that run through a city. There were floating leaves and twigs; pollywogs and minnows; soda bottles and milk cartons. Every once and a while a duck would come paddling down the way.

"Grandpa, where does the water in the creek come from?" Conner asked one day while following Grandpa on his chores in the yard.

"I don't know, Conner. Maybe from a spring," replied Grandpa.

"What's a spring?"

"It's just a place where water comes up from the ground."

"How come?"

"How come what?"

"How come creek water comes up from the ground? I thought water came down from the sky?"

"The rain comes down from the sky and fills up the spring."

"So, the water doesn't come from the spring; it comes from the sky."

"Let's go toss the football around, Conner," concluded Grandpa, abruptly setting down his rake.

Conner, who was curious about everything, suddenly became particularly curious about the water in the creek. Early the next morning, he decided to follow the creek as far upstream as it would go to find the spring where Grandpa said that it started. Conner walked along the grass-covered banks, passing houses and buildings and vacant lots. He passed cars and trucks; children playing and people working in their yards. He even stopped a time or two to chase a random frog or a neighbor's cat along the way. The creek was wide at some places, almost like a small river, and other places it was just a trickle, shallow and full of rocks so that Conner could hop across almost without getting his feet wet.

Almost...

Conner hiked further and further, well beyond where he had ever gone before. As Conner worked his way upstream, the houses and the buildings became fewer and fewer as the creek turned through the countryside into a patch of woods. Here, the banks of the creek became too steep for him to walk along, so Conner climbed up on top of the bank and peered into the woods. He had been hiking for quite a while and really didn't know where he was anymore, but he knew he could find his way home by just following the creek back the way he came. Conner walked on through the woods to see if he could find something that looked familiar, when up ahead he spied a small building standing all alone in a field.

As he got closer, Conner saw that the lonely, brick structure had a big overhead door in the front leading into a garage area. The building seemed to be an old firehouse, kind of like the one he remembered seeing at the Pioneer Town amusement park where Grandpa sometimes took him to play. On the side in big black letters was inscribed "Firehouse No. 9." The old firehouse looked very odd as it stood all alone on no road, with no other buildings within sight. He decided it was something he needed to explore.

Chapter 2

As Conner walked around the front of the old firehouse, the door was open and inside was an old fire engine. It had wooden sides and a big container on the top for water with some hoses wrapped around. Strangely enough, the old fire engine looked new. Not just well-kept like an antique car, or recently re-painted. The fire engine looked fresh from the factory: it was polished and clean, with everything in its place. Conner walked into the firehouse and noticed that the fire gear of all of the firemen from the station was carefully hung on a series of pegs on the wall, each with a name above it:

"Johnson" "Morgan" "Jacobs" "Zachary" "James" "Christian" "Dean" and "Adams".

Beneath the names, there were big red fire hats and coats and boots for each fireman. The clock on the wall read "12:00." Conner's watch read "9:45."

Conner called out, "Hello." There was no answer. "Hello!" he called louder, but no one seemed to be about. Conner peered inside the living quarters of the firehouse and found a kitchen with a table set with eight plates and a platter of fresh biscuits sitting on the kitchen counter and a coffee pot on an old stove with steam rising out of the spout. The room looked like someone had just walked out of it. Conner passed through the kitchen and into the bunk room. He found eight bunks neatly made up, with clothes hanging off of the rail at the end of each.

Conner called again "Hello!" but no one answered.

The firehouse was deserted.

"I wonder who made those biscuits," he thought to himself. As Conner turned to walk out of the bunk room, an alarm suddenly sounded:

"RING! RING! RING! RING!"

Conner jerked around, and to his amazement saw a room now full of firemen scurrying about and putting on the clothes at the ends of the bunks. Conner tried to get the attention of one of them, but the firemen just hurried right past as if they didn't see him at all. The firemen got onto the fire engine, raced out of the garage, and sped across the open field toward the woods.

Conner yelled after them, "Look out, you're going to run into the trees!"

Then, as quickly as they had appeared, the fire engine and all of the firemen vanished into the woods. Conner stared in amazement at what he had just seen. He walked out to where the fire engine had disappeared through the trees, but there was nothing. Not even tracks. They were just gone. Conner wandered through the woods all the way back to the creek. There he sat on the top of the bank and strained to hear the distant sound of an engine, but all he heard was the quiet trickle of the creek.

Conner turned around and walked back to the firehouse. He looked at the old clock on the wall. It still read "12:00." Conner's watch read "10:20." The air was eerily quiet. There was no sound from birds or even from the breeze. Everything was still. Even the clouds seemed to stop moving. Conner shook his head and began to wonder if he really had seen what he thought that he just saw.

Then, without warning, came the sudden roar of an engine bursting out of the silence. Startled, Conner ducked, looking back over his shoulder and saw the fire engine bounding back across the field toward the firehouse. The old engine now had mud on its wheels and its shiny red paint was dirty with soot. Once back in the garage, the firemen each lumbered off the engine, sooty and expressionless, and put up their coats and their boots and their hats, and slowly paced back into the inside of the firehouse.

"Hey, where have you guy's been?" chirped Conner, but no one said a word. No one stopped. No one looked. It was as if Conner wasn't even there.

Conner strode into the firehouse after them, but when he got inside, they were gone. He went into the bunk room, and all of the bunks were back the way they were before: neat and clean, with clothes hanging off of the rail at the end. Conner went back out to the garage, and the fire engine was shiny and clean again. He felt a cool wave flow through him.

"Ghosts! My teacher said there weren't any such thing as ghosts!" Conner walked first around the kitchen, then the bunk room calling:

"Hello! Are you ghosts? Are you ghost firemen?"

No one answered.

Conner sat a long time listening to the quiet of the firehouse and thinking about the firemen. He went back out to the woods again, looking for a clue as to where they had gone, then back into the firehouse. He picked up each of the fire hats and each of the boots, looking for something, anything that might help explain what had happened. With a long sigh, Conner finally decided to go home. He hiked back through the woods, down to the creek and followed it all the way back to the green shutters of home, wondering as he walked, sometimes even aloud, if what he had seen that day was real.

Chapter 3

Conner arrived back home just in time for lunch. He sat down and stared at the ham and cheese sandwich with crinkle potato chips and kiwi fruit drink his Mom had prepared for him.

"Eat, Conner," his Mom said with soft urgency.

"Mom?"

"Yes, Conner."

"Mrs. Evans said that there aren't any such thing as ghosts. Do you believe in ghosts?"

"I don't know, honey. There are a lot of things in this world I don't understand. What do you think? Do you believe in ghosts?"

"I think so. But I thought that they were supposed to be scary and mean."

"Maybe there are good ghosts and bad ghosts. Did you think you saw a ghost?"

"I saw some firemen. I think that they were ghosts. They didn't seem mean, but they didn't talk to me."

"Did they put out ghost fires?" said Conner's mom smiling. Then suddenly she turned and frowned, "Has your Grandpa been telling you ghost stories again?"

"No Mom, I promise," replied Conner with a look of consternation.

"You can talk to a fireman, but remember what I told you about talking to strangers..."

Conner tossed a quick "Yes, Mom" over his shoulder as he ran to his room. He laid on his bed staring at the ceiling and decided to resort to the ultimate authority. Conner hopped up and went down the hallway to Grandpa's room.

"Grandpa?" asked Conner quietly.

"Yes, buddy. What's on your mind," replied Grandpa with a pleasant but serious look. He always knew when Conner was thinking hard about something.

"I think I saw some ghosts today at an old firehouse." Grandpa gazed silently at Conner while he slowly reached around into his back pocket, took a pinch of tobacco out of a little pouch, and put it in his mouth.

"What made you think that they were ghosts, Conner?" Grandpa asked carefully.

"Well, I don't know. They just...appeared and then...

they disappeared," Conner said shaking his head, trying to find the right words to say.

"What kind of ghosts were they?"

"I don't know…they were just firemen."

Grandpa considered Conner's words for a moment, then asked very matter-of-factly, "Did they scare you?"

"No. Not really," shrugged Conner.

"Were they a bunch of old-timer firemen like me?" Grandpa asked with a half-smile.

"No. They were regular firemen, but they wore old fashioned stuff," Conner replied thoughtfully.

"Did you talk to them?" asked Grandpa, leaning his face a little closer to Conner's.

"I tried, but they didn't say anything back," said Conner, his voice giving away a little of the frustration of that part of the encounter.

Grandpa leaned back in his chair, turning away from Conner, and sat still and quiet for a long time just looking out the window. Finally, Grandpa asked quietly, "Are you gonna go back and see them again?"

"I don't know…do you think I should, Grandpa?"

Grandpa hopped up out of his chair as if he were suddenly summoned by somebody, "you do what you think you need to do buddy," Grandpa said leaning over to give Conner a quick kiss on the top of his head on the way by. "You do what you gotta do."

Conner sat up most of the night thinking about the firehouse and the firemen. "I have to go back. I have to see if it really was for real or if I just dreamed it all up."

Conner got up early the next morning, packed his backpack with a day's supply of crackers, a carton of yogurt, a fistful of leftover candy from a friend's birthday party the week before, a map and his "Space Runner" video game.

"Maybe ghosts like video games," he said to himself. "I'm going out to play at the creek, Mom."

"Don't be late for dinner, Conner. Your Grandpa is going to grill hamburgers today," she replied patting him on the head on his way out.

Chapter 4

Conner hiked down to the creek and headed back upstream to the woods. He couldn't tell if it was a lot further than he remembered, or if the anticipation simply was making him impatient to get there.

Finally, he reached the place where the banks of the creek began to get steep as it curved into the woods. Conner ambled up the bank and began hiking through the trees in the direction he remembered. He began to walk faster and faster and finally broke into a run. He stopped at the edge of the woods, and there in the middle of the field was the firehouse, the same as it was yesterday. Conner strode up to the firehouse and found the old fire engine was still in its place along with the hats and boots and coats of the firemen. The kitchen still had fresh biscuits on the platter and hot coffee on the stove.

"Hello! Hello, is anybody here?" Conner called out. No one answered.

The eight bunks were still neatly made with the clothes of each fireman laying across the rail at the end. Conner walked back into the garage area to look at the fire engine. He climbed up on the back to look into the large water tank running his hand along the smooth top. Suddenly, *"RING! RING! RING! RING!"* the alarm sounded. Conner was startled for a moment, and then made a quick decision. He hid down underneath the fire hose. The firemen hopped on the engine and, with a lurch, away they went, racing out of the firehouse and across the field toward the trees.

Conner peeked out from behind the firehose, wincing as they approached the woods. He held his breath, then suddenly, *WHOOSH!!!* There were lights flashing and the sound of wind rushing all around them. Conner looked up at the fireman that was nearest him, but he sternly looked ahead toward wherever they were going. Conner covered up his face and began to wish that he had just gotten out of the way. He wished he had decided to stay home that day. He wished he was still with his Grandpa.

With a jolt, the fire engine broke out of wherever it had been and bounded onto a dusty street. From the fading day light, Conner could tell that it was late in the afternoon. He looked over toward the sound of commotion and he could see other firemen spraying water on a blazing building.

The firemen from Firehouse No. 9 quickly went to work as Conner scurried off of the engine and out of the way. Again, Conner seemed to be completely unnoticed by the firemen. Conner could see that a large building was on fire and up on the roof he could see about five or six children leaning over the side and screaming for help with flames leaping out of the windows below them. Conner heard one of the other local firemen gravely say that the building was blocked off inside and about to collapse and that there was no way to get up there to get the children down. Conner felt a sudden, sharp feeling of desperation grip at his chest as he heard some people crying and others praying.

The firemen from Firehouse No. 9 ran directly through the flames into the building. The smoke was now rising around the children who had all huddled together. In the next instant, the firemen from Firehouse No. 9 appeared on the roof. Scooping up the children their arms, the firemen whisked them off of the roof and back down into the building. A moment later the children all came running out into the street, single file, through the smoke.

Wild cheers rang out, temporarily drowning the noises of the fire. Caught up in the excitement of the moment, Conner forgot about where he was, and when he finally turned around to look back for the firemen from Firehouse No. 9, he was too late. The firemen had all loaded back on the fire engine and were racing back down the street and, before he could call out to them, WHOOSH!…they were gone. The firemen from Firehouse

No. 9 had vanished into the growing dusk as quickly as they had come.

"Uh, oh," Conner exclaimed wide-eyed. He was suddenly all alone, and for the first time, he began to feel afraid.

"I'm not going to cry," he said to himself with resolve, but a tear made its way down his cheek all the same. Steadying himself, Conner walked up to one of the other firemen. "Do you know where I can find Firehouse No. 9?" Conner said trying to sound calm.

"Firehouse No. 9? I don't know of any Firehouse No. 9 around here," said the fireman, barely noticing Conner.

"They ran up on the roof and rescued the children!" Conner urged.

"I don't know how those children got down, son, but there were no firemen up there…we couldn't get through the flames... I don't know how those kids got down," said the fireman shaking his head in disbelief. "It's the darndest thing I ever saw."

Conner was confused by the fireman's answer. He could hear other people talking about how a miracle must have happened for those children to make it down off of that building. Conner pleaded with anyone who would listen that it was the firemen from Firehouse No. 9 that saved them, but people just shook their heads and went about their business.

Conner returned to the fireman he had been talking to. "Where am I?" he asked sheepishly.

"Were you in the fire little boy?" asked the fireman, now looking down for the first time and sizing up the small figure that was standing next to him.

"No, I came on the fire engine from Firehouse No. 9," urged Conner.

"I better take you back to the station with me and try and find out where you live," said the fireman, leaning down and gently putting his hand on Conner's shoulder. Conner climbed into the fireman's truck and rode back to the firehouse. His new friend was a big man and he had a big bump on his cheek.

"What's that?" Conner said pointing to the fireman's face.

The fireman laughed and said, "Chewing' tobacco. It keeps the taste of smoke out of my mouth."

"My Grandpa eats that sometimes. My Mom says it's yucky," Conner remarked making a face.

The fireman chuckled. "I reckon your Mom's right. It is kind of yucky. My wife hates it, too. By the way, my name's Sam, what's yours?"

"Conner," he replied sticking his hand out the way Grandpa taught him. Sam's big hand gently swallowed up Conner's.

"Conner? Hey that's funny, that's my last name. I guess I won't forget you little guy," he said reaching up and rubbing Conner's head affectionately.

Sam drove an old truck, or at least it looked like it should be old, but it didn't look and smell like an old truck. The streets they drove down were sometimes paved and sometimes gravel. The buildings didn't look like the buildings from Conner's town; they looked like the buildings from the older neighborhoods, only in a lot better shape. And the cars that they passed on the road…they all looked like antiques! This was the strangest town that Conner had ever seen.

"What town is this?" questioned Conner anxiously.

"Why, it's Springdale. Don't you know that?" replied Sam, a little incredulous.

"Springdale? That's where I live. I've never been to this part of town before," muttered Conner, looking intently out of the window trying to fix his gaze on something he recognized.

"Don't worry, boy. When we get to the station, we'll find out where you belong. Your folks are bound to be plenty worried by now."

As the truck pulled up to the station, Sam told Conner

to go on into the kitchen and sit down while he and the other firemen put away their gear.

Conner could hear the other firemen talking about the fire and how they couldn't understand how those children got off of the roof. He heard one of them say, "I wonder if it was the good old Ghost Brigade coming to the rescue again?" And they all laughed a tired laugh.

Finally, Sam came in and sat down with Conner. "Okay little guy, do you know your address?" Conner told Sam his name, address and his phone number: "Conner Richman, 3300 Revere Avenue, Springdale. My phone number is 111-555-1616."

"I'm not familiar with that street," said Sam wrinkling his forehead. "And that phone number can't be right."

Conner insisted that he try it. Sam went over to a phone on a desk. It was big and black and had a big dial with numbers in the holes instead of buttons.

"Hello, operator, do you have a 111-555-1616," Sam asked loudly.

"No such number you say? I didn't think so. Do you have a listing for a Richman on a street called 'Revere?'… don't have that either…okay, well thank you, ma'am." Sam looked over at Conner with a frown.

"Young man, I think you need to explain to me where you're really from, so I can get you home."

"That's my name and my address and my phone

number," insisted Conner.

Sam sat looking up and down at Conner trying to decide what to do next. Conner glanced over and saw a newspaper on the kitchen table. The date on the front of the paper said "April 6, 1956".

"Where did you get that old paper?" asked Conner.

"That's the morning paper, son. Quit changing the subject," replied Sam, reaffirming his tone.

Conner thought back to the tunnel with the flashing lights and the whirlwind. Then he thought about how everything looked old but seemed new…and that newspaper! Slowly he began to realize what had happened. "The ghosts went back in time," he said out loud. Conner's eyes became wide.

"What's the matter, son?" asked Sam.

Conner told Sam the whole story about the firehouse and the firemen. Then he showed him his backpack and all the things in it: the crackers, the candy, the yogurt and the video game. Sam looked over each item very carefully and thoughtfully, particularly the Space Runner game. Finally, Conner showed him his map. It was a map of Springdale from his own time. Sam looked at the map in silence for a long time. He squinted at some words that were written down in the corner:

"Copyright 2015," Sam said with a puzzled voice. He sat heavily back in his chair and stared at Conner without saying a word. Finally he asked quietly,

"What did you say the names were that you saw in the firehouse?"

"I don't know if I can remember all of them. There was Johnson, Adams, um, and Jake or something …."

"Jacobs," finished Sam.

"You know about it?" asked Conner excitedly.

"There's a legend," he began. "Nobody really believes it of course, but it's a tale you hear firemen talk about when they are swapping stories. It's about an old fire brigade that was called to fight a big fire at a schoolhouse about forty or fifty years ago. There were a lot of kids trapped inside, and eight firemen rescued them all, but when they went back in one last time to make sure everyone was out safe, the old schoolhouse collapsed, and they were all lost. The legend goes that whenever there are children caught in a fire and can't be saved, the old brigade will come and help rescue them."

Conner and Sam sat and didn't say a word for a long time.

"What do I do? How do I get back home?" Conner finally asked quietly.

"We'll have to wait for another fire," said Sam with sudden resolve. "We'll have to wait until they come back, and then we'll send you back with them."

Sam took Conner home to live with him and his wife in their small house. They didn't have a T.V., but they had a big radio and Conner stayed up and listened to it at night. Conner missed his Mom and Grandpa, but Sam and his wife took care of him like he was their own. They bought him some clothes. They made him read school books they had around the house. They took him to movies and to church with them and they made him eat all the stuff he didn't really like. Sam loved football and he and Conner tossed the ball around every day in the back yard. Conner never knew his real dad, but Sam was just like he imagined his dad would be like. When folks would ask where Conner came from, Sam would just say, "He's our nephew visiting from California."

Days turned into weeks which turned into months. Every night Conner would look out his window at the moon and think about that fateful day at the old firehouse. "I miss you Mom… I miss you Grandpa."

Chapter 5

Then the day came. Sam rushed home, and bursting through the door he announced excitedly, "There's a big fire at an apartment house down in Livingston. This might be our chance." Conner quickly hugged Sam's wife, grabbed his backpack and hopped in the truck. He and Sam raced out of town toward the fire.

"I have a hunch we'll get there in time," offered Sam reassuringly, reaching over to hold Conner's hand.

They could see the smoke from far away and when they arrived, flames were engulfing a large building. They looked up and saw a small girl leaning out of a window on the top floor.

"Our ladders can't get up there!" Conner heard one of the firemen call out. "Keep your eyes open," urged Sam looking down at Conner. Conner looked around to see if he could spot the men from Firehouse No. 9. The situation was clearly getting desperate. Then, suddenly, out of the corner of his eye, WHOOSH! An old fire engine came bounding toward the fire.

"There they are!" yelled Conner.

"Where?" asked Sam anxiously searching the scene.

"Right over there!" shouted Conner, pointing across the street.

"I don't see anything," said Sam looking intently with his hand shading his eyes. Then said, with a look of sudden understanding, "Maybe only you can see them."

"It's them," stated Conner confidently. Then said, hesitating, "I have to go." Conner paused for a moment, looking up at Sam and realizing that he may never see his friend again. "I'll miss you."

Sam leaned down and picked up Conner and gave him a big bearhug.

"I'm gonna miss you too, little guy. You take care of yourself, you hear? Maybe I'll run into you again some day." Then Sam smiled and said, "If you ever see an old man with a wad of tobacco in his jaw and he stops and says howdy to you on the street, it might just be me." Conner gave Sam one more hug, and ran off toward the old fire engine.

"Hey, where's that kid going?" shouted one of the other firemen. "He can't go over there!" He started to run toward Conner to stop him, but Sam grabbed him by the arm. "Let him go. I promise you, he'll be fine. I'll talk to you about it later. Maybe. Just keep an eye on that girl up there."

As they watched, the girl suddenly disappeared from the window and, a moment later, came running out of the building toward the crowd that had gathered on the street. Sam looked over toward where Conner had been running… and he was gone.

Conner climbed up on the fire engine and held on tight. The firemen loaded back on and headed down the street. Soon, WHOOSH!…they were in the tunnel again, and in a few short moments, they landed with a jolt back in the field where Conner had found them. The fire engine slowly pulled into the garage and, once again without a word, without a glance, each of the firemen climbed off of the fire engine, unloaded their gear, and walked back into the firehouse. Conner stood silently and watched them as

they passed. He glanced up at the clock on the wall. It read "12:00."

"I guess it's time for me to go home," said Conner taking a deep breath and releasing it. As he turned around to leave, there was one fireman left standing directly in his path and he was looking straight at Conner. Conner felt himself freeze as the fireman's ghost eyes looked at him.

And then the fireman finally spoke:

"Remember the men of Firehouse No. 9," was all that

he said. Then he walked up to Conner, put his fire hat on Conner's head, smiled, and slowly walked on back into the firehouse. Conner stood motionless, smelling the scent of the old fire hat on his head. He turned to follow the fireman into the firehouse, and he was gone. Then, as if in a dream, the firehouse began to grow hazy. The walls began to become slowly transparent, and, in another moment, it was all gone, vanished, leaving Conner standing all alone in the

field. He reached up and took off the hat. "Firehouse No. 9" it said.

"I'll remember...I'll always remember the men of Firehouse No. 9," Conner whispered quietly. Then he looked up and all around and said louder, "I'll always remember you!" He finally turned and began the long walk home.

Conner looked down at his watch. It read "3:30." He pushed the button to check the date, and even though he had been gone for months, his watch showed that it was still the same date that he left. "I guess I won't be late for dinner after all," he muttered with a smile.

The shadows were growing longer when Conner finally made his way down the creek and back home.

"Where have you been, Conner? And where did you get that hat?" asked his Mom with an animated smile.

"It's a long story and you wouldn't believe me if I told you," Conner exclaimed dramatically as he wrapped his arms around his Mom's waist and squeezed. "I love you, Mom."

"I love you too, honey," said his mom with a lovingly

amused laugh. "Why don't you run outside and see if Grandpa needs any help with the grill."

Conner walked through the house and into the backyard, and there was his Grandpa. Conner stopped on the back step. He watched him move. He looked at the curve of his jaw. Grandpa turned and saw Conner and glanced down at the fire hat he was holding, and a gentle smile came over his face. Conner looked closely into Grandpa's eyes, and he suddenly knew.

"Sam! You're Fireman Sam! You've always been Fireman Sam!"

"Fireman Sam Conner, at your service, little guy," Grandpa said with a formal salute.

Conner ran into his arms

and got the biggest, best hug of his life.

"Why didn't you tell me? I can't believe it! It really is you!" exclaimed Conner, his mind racing.

"It's been my heart's secret for over forty years…and now it's yours, too," said Grandpa quietly.

"Doesn't Mom know?" asked Conner anxiously.

"No one knows, Conner. It's just you and me and you need to promise me that you'll keep it that way," said Grandpa looking deeply into Conner's eyes and holding Conner's hands in each of his.

"I promise," said Conner trying to match the gravity of Grandpa's voice.

"How did all of this happen? What's it all about, Grandpa?" asked Conner, burying his head in Grandpa's stomach.

"The world is full of things we don't understand, boy. The world is full of things we may never understand."
"Tell me about being a fireman, Grandpa. I want to hear

everything."

CPSIA information can be obtained
at www.ICGtesting.com
Printed in the USA
LVHW091535060921
697118LV00014B/256

9 781734 469400